This book belongs to

Andrew Trosato

A Home for Aphie

Published by Advance Publishers
www.advance-publishers.com

Written by Catherine McCafferty
Illustrated by Adrienne Brown and Adam Devaney
Editorial development and management by Bumpy Slide Books
Illustrations produced by Disney Publishing Creative Development
Cover design by Deborah Boone

ISBN: 1-57973-023-X

The ants on Ant Island had a little problem. His
name was Aphie, and he was the Queen's pet. Being
the Queen's pet, he got to do whatever he wanted,
no matter how much trouble he caused.

The Queen and her youngest daughter, Dot, loved
Aphie's antics. The other ants did not.

Atta, Dot's older sister, knew that Aphie was causing problems. He was always tracking mud into Dr. Flora's office or digging up Cornelius's garden. But Atta did not want to scold Aphie. She knew how much Dot and the Queen liked him.

One day, Dot invited Thorny to be a guest speaker at her Blueberry troop meeting.

The Blueberries gathered in Thorny's office with Aphie tagging along behind them.

Thorny began to explain to the Blueberries how to build an anthill. But as Thorny showed them a drawing, Aphie jumped up and licked his face. The Blueberries squealed with laughter.

Thorny tried his best to ignore Aphie. "If you'll look right here," he said, pointing, "you'll see where to build the entrance."

The Blueberries giggled. Aphie had poked his head right through the map!

Later, as the Blueberries were leaving, Dot smiled up at Thorny. "I'm glad we came to see you," she said. "I always thought your work was so serious. But it's fun!"

Thorny sighed and went back to his desk.

The next morning, Atta paid Thorny a visit. She noticed that he looked upset. "How was the Blueberry meeting?" Atta asked him.

Thorny was just about to answer when they heard someone approaching.

Sure enough, the Queen soon appeared with Dot and Aphie. "Aphie can balance a seed on his head!" Dot declared.

Aphie jumped onto one of Thorny's drawings and did his trick. Thorny and Atta clapped politely.

"You're so talented!" said the Queen as she patted Aphie. "You can show Aphie's trick to the Blueberries at your next meeting, Dot."

Dot beamed. "I know. And you should have seen him yesterday, Mother . . ." she began as they left.

Thorny picked up the torn drawing. "Not again! First Aphie ruined the Blueberry meeting yesterday! Now this!" Thorny complained.

"What happened?" asked Atta.

"Aphie kept getting in the way," explained Thorny. "He's got the Blueberries thinking my job is just fun and games! You have to do something! Aphie has got to go!"

Atta and Thorny did not know that Dot was just outside. Dot was coming back to thank Thorny for coming to the Blueberry meeting yesterday. Dot couldn't believe that Thorny wanted to get rid of Aphie. And Atta wasn't stopping him!

Dot tiptoed away with Aphie. If he had to leave, then she would, too. As she reached the main tunnel, she heard Atta call, "Time for bed, Dot."

Dot hugged Aphie. They would run away after everyone fell asleep.

After Dot was in bed, Atta came in and tried to talk to her about Aphie. "Um, Dot, do you think Aphie might be happier living outside?"

Dot squeezed her eyes shut and pretended to sleep.

When Atta left, Dot grabbed her backpack and woke up Aphie. Aphie started to yip.

"Ssshhh!" said Dot. "We've got to be very quiet."

Dot peeked out the door. Then she and Aphie slipped into the hallway.

Once they got outside the anthill, Dot started to feel a little bit scared. It was so dark that she couldn't even see her feeler in front of her face. She and Aphie walked slowly over a hill.

Suddenly there was no ground under Dot's feet!
"Yikes!" Dot cried. She had fallen into a big crack
with steep walls. She wasn't hurt, but she couldn't
climb out. Above her, Aphie scratched at the edge.
Then he settled down to guard Dot.

Back at the anthill, Atta was talking to Thorny again. "What if we built a shelter for Aphie?" she suggested. "We could put it right outside the front entrance. That way, Mother and Dot could still play with him, but he'd be out of our way."

Atta hoped that Thorny would agree. She didn't want to have to make Aphie leave the colony.

"Well," Thorny said finally, "I guess my crew could build a pen for him. But *you* can tell the Queen and Dot about it."

The next morning, Atta hurried to see the Queen and Dot. Something seemed different in the anthill. It was so quiet. Atta found the Queen just outside Dot's room.

The Queen looked alarmed. "Have you seen Dot?"

"I thought she might be with you," said Atta.

"No," said the Queen nervously. "She must be with Aphie."

Atta looked inside Dot's room. She was not there. Neither was Aphie. Dot's backpack was gone, too. Secretly, Atta began to worry.

Just then, Aphie raced into Dot's room, making more noise than ever before.

"He's trying to tell us something," said Atta.
Aphie ran off, with Atta following close behind.

Aphie led Atta to the dry riverbed where Dot was calling for help. Atta quickly saw that Dot was in a narrow crack at the bottom.

"Don't worry, Dot! I'll get help! Aphie will stay with you," Atta called as she flew off.

Atta returned with Thorny and the Queen. Thorny lowered a stalk down to Dot, who climbed to safety.

"Guess Aphie's yapping paid off this time," said Thorny. The Queen hugged her young daughter. "Dot, dear, I thought your Blueberry training taught you not to go outside alone after dark."

Dot knelt down by Aphie and held him close.

"I was out at night because Thorny and Atta said that Aphie had to go!" Dot explained.

"Had to go?" asked the Queen. "Atta, dear, what did you mean?"

Atta looked uncomfortable.

"We meant that, um, Aphie had to go someplace where he wouldn't get into so much trouble," said Atta.

The Queen was surprised. "Trouble? Aphie?"

"Well, he's always digging up Cornelius's garden and tracking mud in Dr. Flora's office. This week he ruined some of Thorny's drawings," she explained.

"But if he can't be inside and he can't be outside near the garden, where can he be?" Dot burst out. Atta smiled at Dot. "How about right in his own special training pen, just outside the entrance?"

Dot wasn't sure. Atta glanced at Thorny for help.
"I'll build him a nice one," Thorny told Dot,
"with lots of room for you to teach him new tricks."
Dot's eyes widened. "Wow!" she exclaimed.
"I could put on shows there, too!"

"Oh, what fun!" said the Queen.

"Wait!" said Dot. "What do you think, Aphie?"

Aphie ran over to Thorny and gave him a big lick on the face.

"Down, bug!" commanded Thorny. He pretended to be mad. But when no one else was looking, Atta saw him smile.

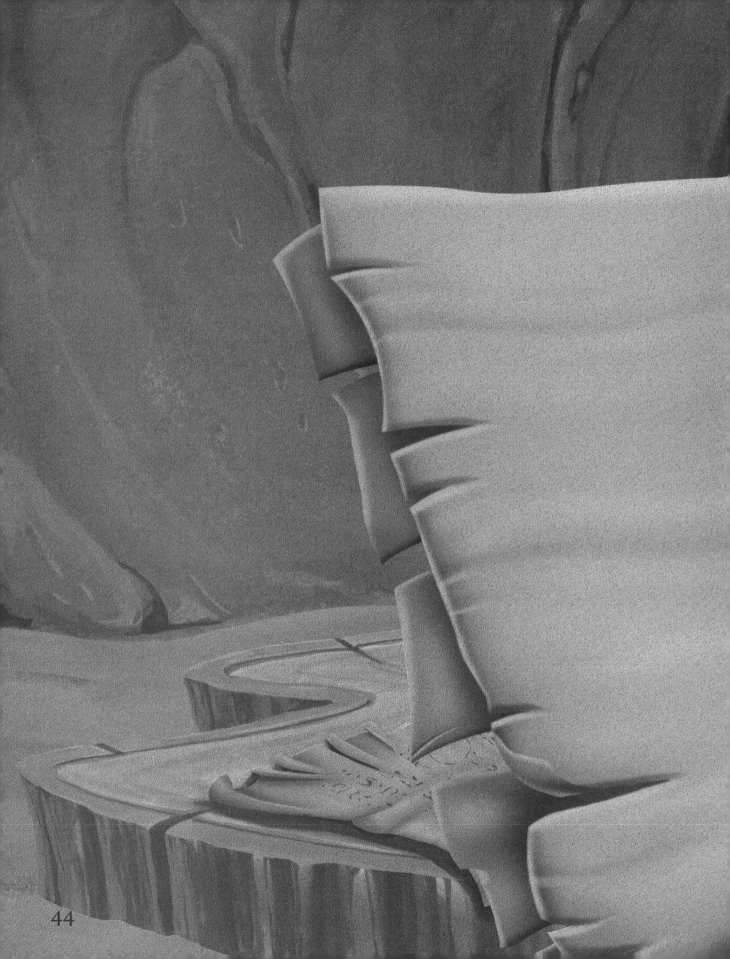

Dear Blueberry Journal,

My mom and I really love Aphie. He's the best pet any ant could have! Mom told me that most times aphids work for ants. She said they make a sweet food called "honeydew" for ants to eat. In return, ants help aphids by keeping them safe from bigger bugs, like wasps. Sometimes ants even build homes for aphids—just like Aphie's pen!

Well, I think Aphie does a lot of work for us even if he doesn't make food. It takes a lot of training to learn those tricks!

Till next time,

Dot